THE HIGHLY CLASSIFIED DOCUMENTATIONS
THAT ARE PRESENTED TO YOU INSIDE OF THIS BOOK ARE FOR EDUCATIONAL
PURPOSES ONLY FOR ALL READERS OF ALL AGES WHOM PURCHASED THIS BOOK
CREATED BY PROFESSOR MCGOKU305 THANK YOU FOR BUYING THIS BOOK

- MCGOKU305 &
 PROFESSOR MCGOKU305

SPECIAL THANKS TO ALL OF MY FANS AND THIS IS THE FINAL VOLUME OF THE
BLACKFACE BOBBY FABLES SERIES OF CHILDREN BOOKS

I Want To Thank Each And Everyone Who Purchased Blackface Bobby Fables Volume Seven
Life Lessons Part 3 & 4
The Final Chapters Was Only Made To Educate The Children Readers And The Adult Readers
On Raising Their Children Better And This Series Dose Contain Dark Elements And Horror
Elements and Violent Themes And Various Situation's That Involves
Scammers , Pick-Pocketers , Tricksters
Profanity Use But It Is Only For Educational Purposes Only

 But They Are Only Added To Let Parents and Children That In Real Life And In The Reality Of
The Present Day That We Live In Today That There Are Evil People In This World That Only
Prey On Children
To Do All Kinds of Wicked and Evil Vicious Things
 And Kidnap Children And Hurt
Children Of Any Age and If Any Parents Are Reading This Now I Want you all To Sit Down With
Your Children An Explain To Them About Everything In This Book
And Please Let Them Know Everything Buy Explaining To Them in a Uncensored Way About
The Dangers If This World And The Dangers Of The Evil People Whom live inside of this World
Pleased Do This To Protect The Lives That You Love
Your Children And Yourself and Never Let Your Child or Children Go Anywhere By Themselves
Without You Around Them a With Them Or Without a Mobile Telephone or a Digital Touch
Screen Telephone Ok
- Professor MCGOKU305

Make Sure To Write Me With Your Fanmail
By Email @

ProfessorMCGOKU305@Gmail.com
ProfessorMCGOKU@Gmail.com

Thank You Kindly My Fans

Blackface Bobby Volume 7: Life Lessons Part Three & Four

Chapter One Beware Of Pick Pocketers

One Day Blackface Bobby Was Coming Home With His Parental Guidance
Mother Blackface From The City
After She Made a ATM Transfer Of $500,000
She Put $1,000 Dollars Inside Of Blackface Bobby's Pocket And

As The Walked and Went Into Another Store To Shop To Purchase grocery And Seeds For
Planting Vegetables

As Blackface Bobby and His Parent Enter The Store Blackface Bobby Asks His Mother a
Question

Blackface Bobby: Mother Is it Okay If I Walk Around and Look Around For a Couple Of Minutes
Mommy
Please Please Please Please Please

And His Mother Replied Back By Saying

Mother Blackface: Well... I Shouldn't Because Of Your Age As a 5 Year Old Adolescent But I
Know You Little Boy Very Well I Carrie You In My Stomach For Nine (9) Months So I Know You
Can Handle Yourself Run Along Bobby and Have Fun and Enjoy Yourself Okay Baby Meet Me
In The Front Of The Store In a Hour Okay Bobby See You Later

After That Blackface Bobby Replies To His Mother By Saying

Blackface Bobby: Okay Mommy Goody Goody Golly Golly I Will Look around Okay Mother Bye

After That Bobby Starts Running Around Happy Go Lucky As He Always Is Then He Looks
Around And Is So Happy and Smiling About His Happiness & Being In a Huge Store Now As
Blackface Bobby Walks Around Casually a Strange Man That Weighs 900 Pounds Stands 5
Feet Tall With a Face That Looks Like a Hook With Eyeballs And Yellow Lips and Web Feet
And Floating Hands And a Deep Dark monstrous Grassy Voice And Large Obese Legs an Feet
He Then Reaches Into Blackface Bobby's Left Pocket
 And Pick Pockets Blackface Bobby For His 1,000 Dollars Now Laughing Then Counting The
Stolen From Bobby's Pocket
and Not Knowing That He Is In aisle 15 Where The Cast Iron Skillets , TNT dynamite and
Baseball Bats
Are at
Meanwhile

As Blackface Bobby Gets Angry An Starts Crying He Then Grabs a 20 inch Cast Iron Skillet Bashes The Pick Pocketer In His Head Then He Takes His Catapult Slingshot and Shoot's Two Rocks In Both Of
 The Pick Pocketers Eyes After That
The Pick Pocketers Falls To The Floor an Starts Screaming & Hollering

Pick Pocketer: Help Help I'm Being Attacked By a Monster. I'm a Victim Please Help Me I'm Being Attacked
By a Monster

 Meanwhile
Blackface Ties Two Sticks Of TNT To Both Of The Pick Pocketers Feet Blackface Bobby Then Grabs His Money Back From
The Pick Pocketer And Blackface Bobby
Leaves The aisle.
Where The Pick Pocketer Is Getting Blowed Up By The TNT Sticks That Are Tied To Both Of His Feet Now
Bobby Is Running To The Front Of The Store Where His Mother Is At and He Starts Yelling

Blackface Bobby: Mommy Mommy a Scammer Is Trying To Rip Me Off For My $1,000 Dollars Please Help

As Mother Blackface Hears This From Her Son and See's Him In Shock She Then
Runs To aisle Where She See's Bobby Coming From The She Grabs Her Sledgehammer From Her Small Purse And Bashes The Pick Pocketer In His Head Five Times Leaving Him Unconscious And delirious And Shaking

And Says To The Pick Pocketer These Words Here

Mother Blackface:
 Look Sucker. This Is The Last and Only Child You Will Ever Pick Pocket In Your Piggly Life You Dang Swine Face Swine Fool You

Meanwhile Then As All Of That Is Going On The Town Police Officer
Officer Dummy Is Looking At Everything From His Car Camera and Enters The Store And Grabs His Hands Cuffs An Places Them On The Pick Pocketer Floating Hands And Officer Dummy
 Tells The Pick Pocketer This

Officer Dummy:

Look Pick Pocketer I Know My Name Is Officer Crash Dummy But You are The Dummy The Dumbest Person In This Case and In Every Case Committing a Crime Is Bad Enough I Do Not Care Whom You Are Committing Then Robbery Crime On a Adult Or a Lion But When You Steal From a Child That Is Low Down And Filthy And Evil Stealing Digitally Or Physically From Any Child Of Any Age Is Wrong And Evil And Is The Worst Thing Ever That Is Why You Are Going In The Pokey and Slammer For Life

Because I Do Not Care How Much You Dislike Or Have A Grudge Against Anyone now I'm not Saying Committing Crimes Or Stealing Is Okay Because It Is Not It Never Okay Nor Is It Good It Is Wrong Alright But You Can Steal Steak , Cake Or a Ex°Lax Milkshake From a Snake But You Cannot Steal For No Child That Is Never Called For That's Why Your Being Apprehended For Grand Theft and grand larceny And Statutory For a Minors Money. You Low Down Dirty Buster Now to Take You To Your Cell Of No Tomorrow At the Crow Bar Motel Your Final Resting Place Forever

Now Let Me Hit You With My
baton Also Known As a
Nail Bat BillyStick

Meanwhile That Is Going On
Mother Blackface And Her Son Blackface Bobby. Start Talking To Each Other

Mother Blackface: Honey My Sweet Little Baby Are You Okay Did He Touch You Anywhere Did He Hit You Anywhere On Your Little Body Because If He Did I Will Give Him a Terrible Beating With My Sledgehammer Right Away
Tell Me Bobby
 Tell Me Bobby
Tell Me I'm Ready To Destroy Him Like A
 Destroyer

And Blackface Bobby Replied Back Saying

Blackface Bobby: No Mother All He Did Was Pick Pocket Me But I Handled Everything With a Cast Iron Skillet and My Catapult Slingshot and Rocks and I Got My $1,000 Dollars Back From Him Too Mommy

Mother Blackface: Few I'm Glad To Hear That Baby I Don't Care About That Money The Amount Dose Not Matter To Me As Long As You Are Alright and Are Doing A Okay My Dear Son I Wish Your Father Was Here But He Was Busy Fixing His Truck and Changing All of The Light Bulbs Inside Of Our House In The Woods Anyways I Fault Myself For Letting You Walk Around This Store Or Anywhere Alone By Yourself Without My Parental Guidance To Guide You Everywhere At This Age Of 5 Years Old That Was Very irresponsible Of Me Rash Of Me. Reckless & Careless Of Me
 And Anything Could Have Happened To You And I Would Have Not Known What I Would Have Done Probably Something Evil With Malicious Things

I Also Blame Myself and
Your Father For Not Telling You About Pick Pocketers I'm sorry Bobby For Putting You in
Danger and By Even Giving You $1,000 Dollars At Your Age Right Now That's Why While We
Are Here I Bought You a Wallet Son But Let Me Reach Right Here In Your Wallet and Retrieve
Your Money $1,000 Dollars and Keep it with Me In the Wallet In My Purse Okay Son

Blackface Bobby: Okay Mommy I Love You

And Mother Blackface Replied Back Saying

Mother Blackface: I Love You Too Lets Go Home and Eat Some Fried Chicken and Watermelon

And Bobby Replied Back Saying

Blackface Bobby: Okay Mama

The End

The Moral & Messages Of This Story
For Parent Readers And Children Readers
Are

Number One

Never Let Your Child Or Children At Any Young Age Walk In The Store Or Anywhere By
Themselves Without Your
Parental Supervision Or The Supervision Of Their Father Or Grandfather Or Grandmother or
Older Brother Or Older Sister Or Older Cousin Please Note That Good Supervision Can Save a
Child Of Any Young Age Life And Never Let a Child Of Any Young Age Out Of Your Sight
Please Mother's Remember This And Please Father's Remember This
 A Child Has Came From Your Bodie's They Are Your Sole Responsibility And They Are Your
Sole Gift Of Love From The Universe And You Must Always Remember That
Never Asked To Come Into This World
They Are Your Duty
They Are Your Bundles Of Joy
They Are Small Version's Of Yourself
And It is Your Life Mission And Job And Career To Protect Them Fight For Them
Feed Them Clean Them And Cloth Them And Most Of All Love Them And Teach Them Right
From Wrong

Number Two

Never Give a Child Something You Know Very Well They Are Not Responsible Enough To
Watch And Keep For Themselves
NEVER AND I MEAN NEVER
PUT OR GIVE ANY CHILD OF A SMALL AGE
Physical Money Or
Credit Cards Visa Or MasterCard
Debit Cards Visa Or MasterCard
 Loaded With Money
 Digital Money From Online Applications (Apps)
Or
 Writable
Check Books or Cheque Books
None Writable
Check Books or Cheque Books

Or. Even House Keyes or Anything That Children Cannot Handle or Be Responsible With Wait
Until Children Are a Certain Smart Mature Age To Handle Things That are For Their
Responsibility

Number Three
Always Watch Everything Your Children Are Doing and Talking Too

 Okay Parents

Those are The
 The Moral & Messages Of This Story
For Parent Readers And Children Readers
Are. Enjoy and Keep Reading Blackface Bobby Fables

Blackface Bobby Volume 7: Life Lessons Part Three & Four

Chapter Two
 The Nice Officer Meets The Blackface Family/Lookout For The Traveling Ponzi Schemers

On Summer Day In July Not a Lie There Once Was a Kind and Jolly Who Wore a Blue Outfit With a Red Tie He Drove a
Paddy Wagon That Look Like A Dragon

And He Was Headed To The
Blackface Families House In The Deep Rural Remote Area Of Georgia To Warn them About The Traveling Ponzi Schemers Who Are Headed In Their Direction And Officer Dummy Wants To Tell Them Before The Scammers Arrive Their

As He Arrives To The Blackface Families House He Smells a Terrible Smell Coming From Their House And He Says

Officer Dummy:
Oh Gosh What The Heck Is That Smell Dog Mess or Hog Mess I Mean Come On Who In The Heck Is Cooking That Mess Is That I Am About Too Vomit Golly Dog Gone What In The Ding Dang World Is Going On Here Nobody's Food Can Smell That Bad Dang it Ugh Thank Goodness This is a Ponzi Scheme and Not a Morthor Case I Would Probably Dry Up If it was Not a Money Scam Case

 As He Walks Out Of His Paddy Wagon
He Goes To The Blackface Families House and Knocks On The Door Three Time and Says

Officer Dummy: Knock Knock Knock
Anybody There Anybody Here
Anybody Where Anybody Hare
This Is Officer Dummy From The Town

After That Father Blackface Comes
From The Kitchen To The Living Room While Holding a Deceased Possum Head In One Hand And Body In The Other Hand
And Answers The Door Saying

Father Blackface: Hi Masa Who Are you Sirs and im Just About To Cook Some Possum and Raccoon and Baboons
And Grisly Bear Meat Want Some Masa and
Who's Are You Looking for Anyways Masta

And Officer Crash Dummy Replies Back Saying

Officer Crash Dummy: Oh Heavens No
No No Sir Mr Blackface That Stuff Stinks I Mean I Must Think You For The Offer But No Thank You I Am Officer Crash Dummy and I Came Here To Tell You All About a Terrible Money Crime Scammer Conmen Known as The Traveling Ponzi Schemers
and I Am Not Your Master I Want To Speak To You & Your Wife

And Father Blackface Says Back To officer Dummy

Father Blackface: Ugh Masta I Mean Sir
I Don't Have a Wife And I Think I Know Who You's Talking About Those Raunchy Schemers Are a Bunch Of People Who Steals Larges Amounts Of Monkey From Various Gullible People Who Are Easy To Be
Quickly Tricked
and Bamboozled
 and Ripped Off
Oh Sir Don't Worry About Me With My Charred Monkey Charcoal Faced Cotton Picking Raccoon Eating
Fried Chicken & Watermelon Loving Blackface Self I Barely Spend Any Monkey I Forget All about Monkey or Any Monkey I Have Sir Are You Sure Your Not Thirsty I Have Some Fresh Tasty Cow Blood in a Huge Picture & Snake Venom In a Glass Bottle Untouched In The Freezer Ready To Drink I Made It Myself From The Cows on my farm and Snakes who live In The Back of my House

And Officer Dummy Replied Back Saying

Officer Dummy: Oh Gosh No Who Drinks That Ahhhhhh? Gosh Darn It Who Drinks That Jazz Blood or Venom That Isn't Good For The Blood System But I Guess Some People Will Drink Anything
Oh My Bloody Gosh I Almost Forgot What I Came Here For Oooh Man
Anyways. I Must Speak To The Women Of The House It Is a Urgent Care

Meanwhile Mother Blackface Rushes To The Front Door To Talk to Officer Dummy and Then She Says

Mother Blackface: Mr Officer Dummy I Remember You .... Sir You Are The Same Police Officer Who Stopped The Fight Between My Son. Blackface Bobby and The Other Child He Told Me All About It And You Apprehended That Pick Pocketer three Months Ago
How Are You Doing I Am So Glad I Am Finally Meeting You For The Very First Time Sir What Brings You Hear to Our Neck of The Woods Please Forgive my Husband He Has Off and On Amnesia But He Is a Very Good Husband and Loving Father. To Our Child

Officer Dummy Replied Back Saying

Officer Dummy: Yes I am That officer I am doing Good Ma'am I am Just Stopping By To Alert You About The Travelling Ponzi Schemers Who Are Headed Here To Where You All Life I Just Came Here To Alarm You On How Crafty They Are On Scamming Any One Even a Child So Please Be On The Look Out For Two Men
Who Are Traveling Ponzi Schemers
That Cannot Run Or Walk Fast
The Two Men
 Are Overweight.
And Dress Like Penguins
And Smoke Cigarette Pipes
And Wear Long Long Necklaces
and Wear Finger Rings
and Wear Wrist Watches
And Drive Oldsmobiles & Road Rollers
And Have Water Guns That Look
 Like Real Pistols
One Man Who Is 1,000 Pounds An Stands 5 Feet Tall and The other Obese Man Is Who Is 2,000 Pounds An Stands 6 Feet Tall
Now That I Have Giving You This Information Use This Wisely and Watch Out For Those Criminals

After that
Mother Blackface
 And Father Blackface
 Both Replied Back to Officer Dummy
Saying

Mother Blackface: Okay Sir Thank You
Father Blackface: Okay Sir Thank You
Mother Blackface: We Will Sir
Father Blackface: We Will Sir

After That Officer Dummy Tells Them

Officer Dummy: Okay Folk I Know You People Will Handle Those Scams Bye You All

And Then mother & father blackface Replies to the officer Saying

Mother Blackface: Okay Sir bye
Father Blackface: Okay Sir bye
Mother Blackface: by Sir

Father Blackface: bye Sir

Meanwhile Blackface Bobby Is in The Kitchen Waiting for His Meal While His Parents Enter The Kitchen They Alarm Him by Saying

 Mother Blackface: Son There Are Two Scam Artists Who Are Coming Near Us Don't Talk To Them Okay Boy

Father Blackface: Okay Sun
Listen to Us We Heard it From Our Officer
Friend That They Are Two Men Who Are Scammers Beware Of Them Son
Mother Blackface: Okay Don't Talk To Strangers
Father Blackface: Okay Don't Talk To Strangers

And After that blackface Bobby Says Back To His Parents

Blackface Bobby: Okay Mama Okay Papa I Will Not Talk To Anyone Who Is a Scammers

Hours Later Blackface Bobby Is Outside In The Woods Playing Basketball With The Wolf's And Foxes And Squirrels And Bears And Rabbits and Hares

As Blackface Bobby
 Dose That And
Dose Those Things With His Animal Friends Two Unknown Objects Show Up
That Are Revealed To Be Oldsmobiles & Road Rollers That Are Being Driven By The Two Traveling Ponzi Schemers
And They Approach Blackface Bobby Saying

Traveling Ponzi Schemers: Hey There Little Boy Don't Be Shy We To Men Are Nice Guys Would You Like To Invest $50,000 Dollars Of Your Allowance With Us On Our Candy Machine Invention
When You Invest $50,000 You Can Make Thousands Of Millions Of Hundreds Of Dollars Back From Your Kind
Investment To Our Invention So Cough Up The Money Or Else Blackie

And Blackface Bobby Replied Back Saying

Blackface Bobby: Your The Ponzi Schemers I Was Warned About Bye Bye

After That Blackface Bobby Pulls Out His
Catapult Slingshot And Shoots Bricks And
Cinder Blocks In The Faces Of The Ponzi Schemers

And The Bobby Throws
 TNT / Dynamite At The Travelling Ponzi Schemers
While He Uses His Mallet To Hit Them in Their Faces As Bobby Takes Very Good Care Of The
Travelling Ponzi Schemers

His Parents And Officer Dummy Are Hinding Behind The Bushes And Officer Dummy Places
His Hand Cuffs On Both Off The Criminals at Once Apprehending Them and Stuffing Them by
Force In His Paddy Wagon and Officer Dummy Says To Bobby and His Parents

Officer Dummy: Thank You All For Everything I Know We Shall See Each Other Again

And the Blackface family Replied Back Saying

The Blackface Family Replied Back Saying

The Blackface Family: Your Welcome Sir

After That The Blackface Family Went Back To Their Happy Lives

THE END

The Morals Of This Story Are

Ponzi Schemers Also Known as
Ripoff Artists Or Scammers Are Online
Or Scam Artists Or Pick Pocketers
Or Simply Scams. are a Very Serious Case In America And All Around The World They Do Not
Care Whom They Beat Out of Money Or Whom They Bother About Their Money They Don't
Care About Anyone Please Beware And Be Aware. Off Scam Artists - Professor MCGOKU305

Blackface Bobby Volume 7: Life Lessons Part Three & Four

Chapter Three
These Kids Are Not Good Part One

One Day Blackface Bobby Was Outside
Playing By Himself After Eating His
Large Breakfast Of
Fried Potatoes
Fried Eggs
Grits
Barley
Alfalfa (Powder)
Fried Chicken
Orange Juice

Whilst He Is
Playing And Playing And Playing Around
With His
Slingshot
And BB Gun Rifle & BB Gun Handgun
TNT Sticks & Dynamite Sticks And His Axe and His Mallet And His Other Explosives That He
Uses For Self Defense Or Playfulness Of Fun Bobby Is Just Coming Out Of The Woods From
Having a Ball By Himself As He Enters Inside Of His House Then Walks Back Outside With His
Small Paper Cup Of Water He Then Starts Drinking The Water From The Cup After Words
Bobby Starts Seeing Shadows Of Children Then He See's Children That He Never Seen Before
And They Ask Him

Neighborhood Children:
 Hey There We Seen You In The Woods Playing Can We Play With You Blackey and Be Your
Friends
Please

And Then Blackface Bobby Replies Back Saying

Blackface Bobby: No I Love Playing By Myself I Got Friends and a Cousin To Play With I Do Not
Know You
Why Would I Want to Play With You Smelly & Dirty Looking Children I Don't Know You Kids
Please Leave

As Blackface Bobby Said That His Parents Over Heard Everything And Before They Could
come To The Outside Good The Children Start To Beg

Blackface Bobby To Play With Him and Then The Parents Come Outside To Tell Bobby To Play With The Neighborhood Kids

Neighborhood Children: Please Play With Us We Want To Only Be Your Friends And Know You

And Blackface Bobby Replied Back Saying

Blackface Bobby: No No way At All You All Smell Like Rotten Fish Gosh Please Leave Now Golly Darn

As The Parents Of Blackface Bobby
Overheard Everything They Started Walking Outside To Convince And Talk To Blackface Bobby About Not Talking To The Children In a Unpleasant Manner Of Name Calling And Bad Manner's

Mother Blackface: Now Boy We Raised You Better Than That To Not Talk DisRespectful To Anyone Apologize Right Now Bobby
Father Blackface: Son If You Think Your Right By Talking To Those Innocent Little Children Whom did not anything To You Boy You Are Wrong Your Getting a Whipping This Instance If You Don't Apologize To Those Children and Let them Play with You Okay Boy

Then Blackface Bobby Replied Back To His Parents Saying

Blackface Bobby: Okay Mother Okay Father I Will Never Be Mean To These Kids or Any Kids Ever Again and Hey I'm
Sorry For Talking Mean to you Kids Lets be Friends and Will You Accept My Apologies

And The Children Replied To Bobby Saying

Neighborhood Children: Okay Apologies Accepted Lets Play and Have Fun

And Blackface Bobby's Parents Said

Mother Blackface: That's Good
Very Good
Father Blackface: Bobby Has Some New Friends

Weeks Later After Blackface Bobby Was Enjoying Himself Having New Friends
His Parents Pull him to the side and have a talk to him about those children he plays with

Mother Blackface:
This time I Am Going To Let You Play With Them Okay Sweet Little Baby
But
Your Not like them
Your Different From Them
Your Life Will Be Completely Beautiful And Different From Theirs Okay Baby
When You See Them Be Nice To Them And Friendly With Them At The End Of The Day
They Are Still Somebody's Children Okay Blacky

Father Blackface: In Other Words Son
We Can See The Things That You Cannot See Because Your a Child And We Are Your
Parents The Adults and Son It Is Our Job To Guide You In The Right Way And Not The Wrong
Way We Can See That
And We Really Do Not Want To Say This But We Can See That Sooner Faster Or Later In
Those Children's Life's That They Will Be Going Down A Terribly Bad Road
Ok Son Remember What We Said

As Blackface Bobby Listens To Each Words His Parents Says To Him He Then Replies Back
To His Parents By Saying

Blackface Bobby: Okay Mommy Okay Daddy

And The Next Couple Of Days
As Blackface Bobby Is Playing With The Same Children He Met
 While His Mother Is Shopping Inside Of The Store Bobby Is Outside Playing Tag Then Hide
And Seek With The Little Children But As Blackface Bobby Is Having a ball
 With The Children
 He Is Now
Understanding What His Parents Told Him
And His Is Witnessing These Same Children Opening The Car Doors Of. Innocent Various
Shoppers In The Store
And Before They Could Attempt To Open The Car Door Of Blackface Bobby's Mother's Car He
Stops Them By Jumping In Front Of Them Blocking Them From His Mothers Car And Yelling
These Words

Blackface Bobby: STOP STOP STOP NOW
HALT STOPPPPPPP!

And The Children Stop And Blackface Bobby Runs Into The Store Telling His Mother Everything
And She Replies Telling Him

Mother Blackface: Well Son That Is What Me And Your Father Were Trying To Explain To You That These Children. Are Going Down a Terrible Road and They Are No Good To Play With Or Be Around They Are a Bad Influence For You Son

And. Blackface Bobby Replied Back Saying

Blackface Bobby: Okay Mama I Love You

Mother Blackface: Okay Son I Love You Too Lets Go Home And Eat Some Vegetable Soup And Peach Pie

Blackface Bobby: Yummy Yummy Mommy

After That Blackface Bobby Never Seen Those Children Ever Again Because They Were Doing Time In The Juvenile Pokey Center For Breaking Into Cars And Shoplifting From Stores

THE END

The Morals And Messages Written Within And Inside Of This Story For The Children And Parents Reading This Book

Lesson One
As a Parent You Can See What Kind Of Influence That Are Around Your Children Or Child Because As A Parent You Can See Things That They Cannot See And Hear The Things That They Cannot See

Lessons Two
If You See Your Innocent Children Playing Around Or Becoming Friends With Children That Are A bad Influence and They Start Acting Or Their Behavior Changes Drastically Different From How You Originally Raised Them You Need To Stop You Children Right Away From Being Around Them Immediately

This Is From Professor MCGOKU305

Blackface Bobby Volume 7: Life Lessons Part Three & Four

Chapter Four
These Kids Are Not Good Part Two

Months Later After Blackface Bobby's Parents Stopped Him From Playing With Those Horrible Children He Meets a New Batch Of Children That Pop Out Of Nowhere As Himself and His Parents Are Out Shopping For Various Items From The Mall In The City

And This Time These New Children And Teenagers Are Using Profane Words That Are Filled With Profanities That Blackface Bobby Never Used Before And Was Advised To Never Use and Bobby's Parents Watched Him From The Other End Of The Store To If He Would Still Talk With Them After Hearing Them Speak With Such Filth In The Young Mouths And Blackface Bobby Walks Away From Them Saying

Blackface Bobby: Bye I Don't Talk To Potty Mouth Like You Bye Bye
My Mommy And My Daddy Taught Me Better Then Yours Did I Was Raised To Never Talk To Anyone That Uses Profanities In Their Speech

And As Blackface Bobby Walks To His Mother and Father They Said To Him

Mother & Father Blackface:
We Are So Proud Of You Son Let Us Finish Shopping

And Blackface Bobby Replied Back Saying
To His Mother And Father

Blackface Bobby: Ok Mommy Ok Daddy

The End

Morals and Message Of This Story

Always Teach Your Children To Never Use Profanities Or No Bad Words And To Never Smoke Cigarettes Or Drink Alcohol
Because Those Are Horrible Things For Anyone To Do

- Professor MCGOKU305

Blackface Bobby Volume 7: Life Lessons Part Three & Four

Chapter Five Do Not Help That Snake & Spider He Or She Will Bite You For Being Kind

Once Upon a Time There Was a
Obese Cat And Rat And They Were Going Inside Of The Supermarket To Shop
The Obese Cat Was Shopping For Fish &
The Rat Was Shopping For Cheese
As They Both Leave Their Cars And Before They Can Enter The Supermarket Good They Encounter
 Two People a Green Reptile Name
Scam The Snake And a Black arthropods Bug Name Luck Ripoff Stink Spider
Who Are Begging Them For Money To Purchase Food and As They Beg
The Obese Cat And The Rat
The Rat Ignores Them While
The Obese Cat Tries To Ignore Them But
Fails And As He Is about To Give Them Food His Friends The Rat Stopped Him For a Minute
By Telling Him Twice In a Nicey Spicy Way

The Rat: Look Cat What Do I Must Do Hit You With a Baseball Bat If You Help That Snake He Will Not Give Or Buy You a Piece Of Cake He Will Bite You Smite You Or Worst Hit You With a Rake For Heavens Sake What Time Did You Awake Yesterday Or Today This Reptile And That arthropods Are Trying To Take Your Luck and Common Sense and Good Living From You Its Not Your Food and Money That They Want It is Your Life They Want Watch Now They Will Attempt To Look Pitiful And Saddened But Don't Let Those Fraudulence Fake Faces Two You They Are Not Really I Need Of Help They Want You To Be a Fool For Them a Ignorant Fool and a No Sense Fool For Them Please Whatever You Do Please Do Not Give Them Your Food Or Money. because They Will Bite You Okay My Friend

And As The Obese Cat Listens To The Rat He nods his head back and forth
From East To North And Replies Back To The Rat Saying These Words

The Obese Cat: LOOK HERE!!!!
You muroid Rodent. I Don't Tell You How To Cook Your Cheese and Eat It And You Don't Tell Me How To Fry My Fish and Catch It Or Eat It I Can Help Anyone I Want Whenever I Want And You Can't Stop Me What Kind Of Friend Are You Telling Me Not To Help These Poor Kind People You Should Be. Ashamed Of Yourself Shorty With Those Buck Teeth Darn You

And The Rat Replied To The Obese The Last and Final Time and Says These Words

The Rat: Well I Am a Friend a Caring Friend That is What Friends Do Alarm The One Whom Is Not Automatically Alarmed When they Are in Serious Danger But Always Remember a Fool And

Their Money Shall Soon Departed From One Another and a Mule And His Food Shall Soon Departure Okay My Friend Let Me Shoppe For My Delicious Food

And As The Rat Goes Into The Store To Shop He Then Leaves The Obese Rat To Deal With His Own Foolishness

Now That The Obese Cat Is About To Give His Food and Money To The Snake and Spider The Two Begging Animals Start
To Look Pitiful And. They Start To Look Saddened And As The Obese Cat Gives Them First His Money Their Faces Start To Look Maddening They Are No Longer Covered In Their Hooded Robes And As The Obese Rat Gives Them His
Fresh Cooked Seasoned Red Snapper Fish From His Pocket They Start Looking
At Him Angry For Giving Them His Food and Money and Now They Pull Out Swords And Bricks To Hit and Kick the Obese Cat And Then

The Obese Cat Starts To Run and. tried
To Hide Then He Goes Under His Car Then Slides To The Other Side and Sees The Snake Whose Attempts To Bite and Smite Him And Beat Him With a Rake He Runs From The Snake and He then See's The Spider Whose Body Has Gotten Wider And Takes a Hammer and Tries To Hit The Obese Cat In His Head But Fails As The Obese Cat Is Scared and Frightened He Taps Into a hidden Strength That Was Buried Deep Within Him He Then Transforms From a Obese Cat Who is Crying Into a Angry Ferocious Lion That Screams and Yells And Tells The Spider

Super Lion:
You Fool I am Not That Obese Cat I Am Super Lion Who is Going To Make You Start Crying

 As Hearing That The Spider Tried To Run
The Same Spider Tries To Hide But Nothing He Dose Work He Cut in The Arm By The Lions Claw and He Is Hitted in The Head By the Avil The Lion Dropped Upon His Head Then The Snake Tries To Hit The Super Lion With a Brick Cake. But Before He Dose That
The Obese Cat's Friend The Rat
Whacks The Snake In The Heid With His Baseball Bat And Makes Them Scat But Not Without Retrieving The Money From The Snake and Spider That they Suckered From The Obese Cat After That
The Obese Cat Returns to His Normal State Without Bitterness Or Hate For Those Two People The Snake And Spider
 Who Did Him Wrong
He Then Puts His Money Right Back Into His Pocket And He Then Strongly Punches The Snake and Spider Into Another Dimension Never Seeing Them Again

And The Obese Cat Apologies To
The Rat By Saying

The Obese Cat: Look Ratty Buddy Ole Pal I'm Sorry For Talking To You Rough Like That I Didn't Actually Know People Are False Like That In The World I Thought Everyone Was Honest and Nice But Some People Are and Some People Are Not
Will You Please Accept My Apologies I'm Really Sorry Friend

And
Then The Rat Replies Back To The Obese Cat By Saying

The Rat: Of Course Buddy No Bad Feelings You Know You Had To Learn This Life Lesson The Hard Way Because There Is No Easy Way Of Learning That People Are Bad But There Are People That Are Good But Look You Are Not a Charity Or a Donation House For Everyone In The World Just Do Not Help People Okay My Friend

And The Obese Cat Replied Back Saying

The Obese Cat: Okay Great

The End

The Moral and Message Of This Story Is
To Advise And Let No One Have Your Money Or Food Because That Is The Pure Jinks. (Jinx) And Bad Luck To Anyone Who Dose So. - Professor MCGOKU305

Blackface Bobby Volume 7: Life Lessons Part Three & Four

Chapter Six Blackface Bobby Goes To School Part One

One Day After Summer Of Cucumber Slumber Blackface Bobby Starts His First Day Of School At Drummer School For Kids and The Morning The Bobby Wakes Up He Goes To The Kitchen To Eat Some Supper
Cheese Grits And Fried Eggs And Fried Raccoon Barbecue Chicken And Watermelon And Gun Powder Cereal
His Favorite Meal For Breakfast Food

Before Bobby's Parents Take Him To School They Both Inform Him About Where He Is About To Attend By Telling Him

Mother Blackface: Look Son This School We Are Taking You Too Is Full Of Various Children Who Have Various Energies upon them Respect Your Elders Okay Bobby

Father Blackface: and Son Here is Something That You Must Know If Anyone Hits You On Any Part Of your Body You Beat Them Up Until You Cannot See Them Anymore Okay Son

Mother Blackface: That's Right Son Give Them A Whipping And a Lashing That They Deserve And Call Us And We Will Come And Give The Heck To Pay My Baby
We Will Give You The House Phone Number So You Can Call Us Anytime You Need Us Okay Son And
Only And Only If They Hit You First Son and Remember Keep Your Hands To Yourself And Never Touch Anyone Unless The Touch You In a Vicious Way. Or on a Uncomfortable Part Of Your Body Okay Bobby
And Son I Don't Care If The Person Is a Teacher Of Your's Or janitors Or custodian Of The School. Or another School Student (Child)
If They Touch You Anywhere Viciously &
Uncomfortable Beat The Living Heck And Hades Out Of Them Keep Your Mallet And Slingshot And Bricks In Your Backpack And Pocket Honey
And Call Us Right Away Bobby We Are Coming And Remember Son This Main Thing From Us

Mother Blackface & Father Blackface:
You Can Always Tell Us Anything That's Bothering You And When Anyone Is Bothering You Our Child..

And After Blackface Bobby Replies To His Parents By Saying

Blackface Bobby: Ok Mommy Okay Daddy I Will

Afterwards Blackface Bobby Is Riding In The Backseat Of His Parents Car Travelling To His First Day Of School

As The Blackface Family Pulls Into The Drive Way and Enters Into a Parking Space Safely Then They Take Blackface Bobby Into The School To Register Him Into The System And Then Take Him To The Classroom Where He Meets The Other Teacher and Other Children

Blackface Bobby Volume 7: Life Lessons Part Three & Four

Chapter Seven Blackface Bobby Goes To School Part Two

As Blackface Bobby Is Introduced To The Teachers And The Children Bobby He Then Sits
Down In The Chair Desk and His Parents Leave And Afterwards Blackface Bobby Is Handed a
Book By The That Has Mathematics Inside Of It And Blackface Bobby Dose Not Know How To
Count Nor Dose He Know What The Numbers Were Inside Of The Mathematics Book As The
Teacher Passes By Each Student And See's All Of The Other Boys and Girls Understanding
Everything Within The Math Book And The Teacher Notices That Blackface Bobby
Dose Not Understand Anything In
The Math Book So The Teacher Asks Blackface Bobby About The Book By Saying

Teacher: Bobby Do You Understand Anything In the Book

And Blackface Bobby Replied Back Saying

Blackface Bobby: No Ma'am What Kind Of Book Is This I Understand The Letters And
Everything Else Accept The Other Parts Of This Book Ma'am

And The Teacher Replied Back Saying

Teacher: Bobby I Will Help You Understand How To Count And I Am Glad
That You Know How To Spell And Read Letters But Bobby I Will Teach You How Count The
Numbers In This Book
The Numbers Are One & Two & Three Four And Five And Six And Seven And Eight And Nine
And Ten Now Repeat Them Back To Me Blackface Bobby And Remember Bobby As Long As
You Can Read Letters You Can Count Numbers On Your Hands And In Your Head And On
Your Paper With Your Ink Pen Always Remember That Little Boy Okay Bobby

And Blackface Bobby Replied Back Saying

Blackface Bobby: Thank You So Much Ma"ma Your a Good Teacher The Numbers Are One
And Two And Three And Four And Five And Six And Seven And Eight And Nine And Ten Did I
Say Them Right Ma'am

And The Teacher Replied Back To Blackface Bobby Saying

Teacher: Yes My Student You Counted Them And Said Them Perfectly Well

After That And Doing a Long Day Of School Blackface Bobby's Parents Are Arriving At His
School To Pick Him Up But Before His Parents Can Get To The Classroom To Pickup Bobby
His Teacher Pulls Them To The Side and Asks Them This

Teacher: I Must Ask You This From a Learn Point But Did You Ever Teach Blackface Bobby How To Count His Numbers Now Don't Get Me Wrong His Is a Very Intelligent Young Man And Is Very Great at Reading and Writing And Spelling And Pronouncing His Words And Letters And All Of The Thing's That Are Placed In Front Of Him But The Only Problem Is That He Lacks The Skills and Knowledge Of Counting His Words Now Is It Okay If I Personally Teach Him Every Day Here At School Before Class Starts and Before Lunch Time and After Class His Mathematics If That Is Fine With You

And Blackface Bobby's Parents Reply To The Teacher By Saying

Mother Blackface & Father Blackface:
Oh Man We Forgot To Teach Him How To Count His Numbers And Yes It Is Okay For You To Teach Him How To Count You Have Our Permission

And The Teacher Replied Back Saying

Teacher: that Is Great I Will Start Teaching Him First Thing Tomorrow Morning

Afterwards Blackface Bobby's Family Retrieve Him From School And Take Him back Home To Eat

Blackface Bobby Volume 7: Life Lessons Part Three & Four

Chapter Eight Blackface Bobby Goes To School Part Three

After A Whole Week Of Blackface Bobby Getting His Mathematics Lessons From His Teacher He Then Is Learning Much Better And Better and Is Now a Perfect Student Of The Mathematics He Knows His Subtractions and Time Tables And Other Forms Of Mathematics Thanks To His Teacher. And That Is The End Of This Story The End

The Morals And Messages Of This Story
For The Readers Of This Book

Hi There If Your Children Or Grandchildren
Are Having Trouble Reading , Writing Or Counting And Spelling Take Time Out To Teach Your Children To Teach Them The Fundamentals Of Education That They Truly Need In Their Young Lives
- Professor MCGOKU305

Blackface Bobby Volume 7: Life Lessons Part Three & Four

Chapter Nine Blackface Bobby Meets
The Obese Cat And The Rat But Don't Be Fooled At All Part One

One Time On A Extremely Windy Day Blackface Bobby Plays In The Hay As Much As He
Wants Soon After Blackface Bobby Is Smelling a Loud Delicious Smell Of Roasted Cheese And
Roasted Fish
Now As Little Bobby Is About To Follow The Smell He Walks Into a Shell From a Snail That
Contains A
 Cheeseburger
And French Fries And Smothered In Onions As Blackface Bobby Ate it He Became Full And
Sleepy and Started To get Leapy Because He Had Ate From That Shell On a Snail As
Blackface Bobby Burped All Of The helium celsius flatchulance From His Stomach and Is
Feeling More Healing. Much Better After That Blackface Bobby Follows His
Nose (Nasus) Walks And Into The Woods Until He See's What He Has Smelled and He Heard
a Yell From a Tree Telling Me

Tree:
Go Back Home To Back Home Leave This Area Alone Little Boy
Go Back To Home Go Back To Home
Leave This Area ALone Go Back To Home

And After Blackface Bobby Hears The Tree Warning Him He Still Keeps Walking Into The
Forest And What He Found Was a Bunch Of Two Animals That Are
A Obese Cat And
A Rat. That Are Roasting Cheese and Fish on a Open Fire on Wooden Logs

Blackface Bobby Asks The Obese Cat a Question

Blackface Bobby: Hey There Mister Cat My Name Is Bobby May I Have Some Of That Fish You
Have There Cooking Sir

And The Obese Cat Replied Back To Blackface Bobby Saying

Obese Cat: Sure Sure But First You Have To Do Something For Me In Order For Me To Give
You Some Of That Fish I Am Roasting Blacky

And Blackface Bobby Replied Back Saying

Blackface Bobby: Ok Sir What Must I Do

And The Obese Cat Said

The Obese Cat: Go Over There inside Of That Bear Cave and Pull One String of Hair From The Mother Bear and Papa Bear. As They Both Sleep They Won't Feel Anything Because Bears Can't Hear or Feel Anything While They Are asleep After That Step On The Sleeping Alligator's Eye He Won't Feel it Either And After Your Done With All Of That Then You Can Get Yourself Some Of That Fish of mines Okay Little Black Boy

And Blackface Bobby Replied Back Saying Okay Mr Obese Cat

Afterwards Blackface Bobby Is Confronted By The Rat With Verbal Words

The Rat: Don't You Listen To Him Can't You See He is Just Trying To Scam You Out Of Your Precious Time Kid He Is a Trickster And Kickster and Hipster
a No Gooded Tyrant Just Don't Be Fooled By The Fooler of Foolery

And Blackface Bobby Replied Back Saying

Blackface Bobby: Oh Mr Rat I Don't Believe a Word You Say Mr Obese Kitty Would not lie To me Or Trick Me He is Just a Animal What Dose He Know about Lying To a Little Child Like Me

And The Rat Replied Back To Bobby

The Rat: Well. Suit Yourself Boy
Your In a Rule Of Waken Little Black Boy Blackface Bobby Blacky

After That and Not taking Heed to the Feline Blackface Bobby Is Heading into the Extremely Pitch Dark Cold Quiet Pitch Black Roaded Bear Cave Where The Bears Live At

Blackface Bobby Volume 7: Life Lessons Part Three & Four

Chapter Ten Blackface Bobby Meets
The Obese Cat And The Rat But Don't Be Fooled At All Part Two

As Blackface Bobby Is Going Inside Of The Bear Cave He See's a Small Bear Cub and He Then Pulls a String Of Hair From His Head Then He Walks a Little More and See's A Large Black Snoring Pillow That He Bumps Into Now He Learns That Is The Mother Bear and He Then Pulls a String Of Her Hair And Afterwards He See's Father Bear and Then Bobby Pull's a String Of His Hair From His Head After That Blackface Bobby Smells A Delicious Smell From The Bears Kitchen So Blackface Bobby Walks In Their To See What Is Smelling So Good To His Little Nose and He Then Learns That It Is Three Bowls and a Large Black Pot With a Pair Of Eyes and Nose and a Mouth Full Of Chocolate & Honey , Molasses Banana Nut
 Oatmeal And Blackface Bobby Sits In The Large Chair Of Father Bear and Eats All Of The Oatmeal and Then Sits In The Medium Size Chair Of Mother Bear Eats All Of Her Oatmeal And Then He Sits in The high chair That for The Baby Bear And Eats All Of His Oatmeal and After That Blackface Bobby Is Going To The Large Black Pot That Has Eyes And Ears And A Mouth and Hands and as Blackface Bobby Opens Up The Lid Of The Pot He Retrieves a Large Spoons and Starts To Eat All Of The Food And After Blackface Bobby Is Then Finished and Is Successfully Done Eating All Of The Oatmeal Not. having Much Knowledge That The Refrigerator Contains Tons Of Oatmeal He Is Then Seen Climbing Down The Latter To The Leave The Bears Cave With The Strings Of Hair Not Without The large Black Pot Screaming and Yelling These Words

The Large black Pot: Help Help Help I'm Empty a Thief Has Eating All of The Oatmeal From Me Help Me Help Me Help Me Please I Repeat a Thief Has Eating All of The Oatmeal From Me

After Blackface Bobby Hears That He Looks at The Pot and Asked Him This Question Before Leaving The Bears Cave

Blackface Bobby: Mister Talking Black Pot What is a Thief is That a Cat

And The Large Black Pot Is Replied Back Saying

The Large Black Pot: Little Boy
A thief Is a Person Who Steals Thing's That Dose Not Belong To Him And A Thief Is a Very Bad Person That Can Be a a Man Or a Woman
A Male Or Female
A Boy Or Girl
A Adult Or Child
A Cat Or Dog
A Rat Or Hog
A Bat or Frog

Whom They Or Who They Are Dose Not Matter a Thief. Is a Terrible Terrible Person That Is a Extremely Filthy Hearted Spirit
You See Little Black Boy
The Definition Of a
Thief Is
Also Known As Thief. or highwayman
the action or crime of stealing That Person Is Going To The Pokey For Life
Now Run A Long Before That Thief Finds You Little Black Boy

And Blackface Bobby Replied Back Saying

Blackface Bobby: Okay Sir Thank You For Telling Me

And Then Blackface Bobby Runs Out Of The Cave With The Bears Chasing Him Until Blackface Bobby Jumps Into a Tree and Then Falls upon The Tip Top Of The Alligators Head And Not Knowing What a Alligator Even Is Blackface Bobby Asks The Two Eyes He is Talking To This Question

Blackface Bobby: Hi Mr Eyes Can you Tell Me Where Can I Find The Alligator At I Was Told By a Obese Cat To Step On The Alligator's Eyes Because Alligators Don't Feel Anything When They Are Asleep
Nor Can They Hear Anything When They Are Asleep

And The Alligator Replied Back Laughing and Went To Holding blackface bobby in his Hand

The Alligator: Haha haha Haha Haha Haha haha haha haha haha haha haha hahaha haha haha haha haha hahaha hahaha hahaha hahaha haha haha haha haha haha haha haha Look Little Boy
I Am a Alligator The Same Alligator That The Obese Cat Told You To Step On Eyes Now I Can Feel and Hear Anything That Is Going On Around Me Alright Child Now Lead Me To Where The Obese Cat Is At Child

And Blackface Bobby Replied To The Alligator Saying

Blackface Bobby: OK Sir Let Me Take You To Mr Obese Cat

As Blackface Bobby Rides On Top Of The Alligator Back They Both Are Traveling To Where The Obese Cat And The Rat Are
At Roasting Their Cheese and Fish On a Open Fire

As They Both Are Their Where
The Obese Cat

And The Rat Are At

The Alligator Tells Bobby This

The Alligator: Hey There My Boy let Me Take This PussyCat Around This Corner Behind The Tree To Talk To Him For a Minute

And Blackface Bobby Replied Back Saying To The Alligator

Blackface Bobby: Okay Sir

As The Alligator Grabs The Obese Cat By The His Hand He Then Takes Him Around His Corner Behind The Tree and You Can Hear The Obese Cat Being Punched and Kicked And Slapped And Whipped Up and Down and As The Alligator And The Obese Cat Has Two Black and Blue Eyes
And Bruises All Over His Body

And The Alligator Is Smiling After Having Revenge On The Obese Cat And The Alligator Sits Bobby Down And Tells him these important Life Lessons And Asks Him Questions

The Alligator: Now Bobby I Do Not Care Who Tells You Something To Do
To Someone Else That You May Know Of Or May Not Know Of or Never Seen Before That Gives You No Reason To Do It I Don't Care What They Tell You They Will Give You In Return Or Will Do For You For Doing It That Person Is Up To No Good Bobby You Should Always Ask These Questions
Why Do I Have To Do That To That Person
 Who Are They
What Did They Do To Me
What Did They Do To You
Are You Mad at Them
Are They Mad at You
Are You Mad At Me

And Then Again Bobby All You Have To Do Is Just Say This

No I Will Not Do That You Do Not Have
Any Control Over Me I Have Control Over
My Mind Over My Actions Over My Life
Over everything That I Do Or Say & Live
I Have Full Control Over Myself I Love Myself I Will Never Harm Myself Over Anyone or Anything Nor Will I Harm Anyone For You Okay Goodbye Soon Long and Farewell Forever

Okay Bobby Now Let Me Ask You Something Dis This Obese Cat Tell You by Any Chance That He will give You Some of That Fish After You Stepped into my eyes

And Blackface Bobby Replied Back Saying

Blackface Bobby: Yes He Did Mister Alligator Sir He Sure Did but Please Forgive Me I didn't know What I was About To Do Was Wrong I'm sorry that will never happen again

Meanwhile Blackface is Apologing To The
Alligator The Same Grisly Bears Who Think A Thief Has Eating All Of Their Steaming Chard Hot Oatmeal Is on The Loose They Are Using The Smell On The Earth To Track Down The Thief So They Can Give Him a Piece Of Their Minds

And As That Is Going On Blackface Bobby Continues To Say To The Alligator

Blackface Bobby: Sir i Had No Idea I Was Being Fooled By Him Honest I'm So Sorry I'm So Sorry I Feel Very Bad About That

And The Alligator Tells Bobby These things

The Alligator: Now That You Learned Better You Know Better and You Know Now To never Do Those Kinds of Things in The First Place Like I Said Before I Do Not Care Whom It Is Bobby It Can Be Your Very Own Parents Almost Anyone Can Steer. You In The Wrong Direction In Life But It Takes One Person Who Can , Could Would and Will steer You Or Anyone in the right direction Of Life Okay Boy Always Remember That Young Child Okay Run Along With This Roasted Fish And Chesses These Two Chimps and Chumps Can fend for themselves Even Though The Rat Had Nothing To Do With It He Could Have Clobbered This Obese Cat With a Nail Bat To Stop Him
Haha Haha Haha Run Along Little Boy With These Goods and Remember What I Said

And Blackface Bobby Replied Back Saying

Blackface Bobby: Okay Sir Thank You And I Will Always Remember What You Told Me Mr. Alligator Sir Thank You Very Much Sir Thank You Very Much Sir

After That The Grisly Bears Have Found The Obese Cat and Beated Him Up

And Blackface Bobby Has Learned a Valuable Life Lesson

The End

The Morals And Messages Written In This Story

Within This Story Blackface Bobby Learns To Not Do Bad Things That The Obese Cat Or
Anyone Tells Him To Do But
This Message Goes For Anyone Not Just The Children For Adults and Teenagers And anyone
Please Take Heed To This Message And Learn From It

 - Professor MCGOKU305

Blackface Bobby Volume 7: Life Lessons Part Three & Four

Chapter Eleven

Joy And Love And Happiness
A Nursery Rhymes Written By MCGOKU305

Joy And Love And Happiness
 Joy And Love And Gladness
Joy And Love And Peace
Joy And Love And Fun
Joy And Love And Love
Joy And Love And Mist
Joy And Love And Joy
Joy And Love And More Joy
Joy And Love And Regal
Joy And Love And Love Joy
Joy And Love And Beauty
Joy And Love And Beautiful Life
Joy And Love And Happiness
Joy And Love And Laughter

Chapter Twelve
Mathematics For Children Part One

1+1=2
1+2=3
1+3=4
1+4=5
1+5=6
1+6=7
1+7=8
1+8=9
1+9=10
1+10=11
1+11=12
1+12=13
1+13=14
1+14=15
1+15=16
1+16=17
1+17=18
1+18=19
1+19=20
1+20=21
1+21=22
1-22=23
1+23=24
1+24=25
1+25=26
1+26=27
1+27=28
1+28=28
1+29=30
1+30=31
1+31=32
1+32=33
1+33=34
1+34=35
1+35=36
1+36=37
1+37=38
1+38=39

1+39=40
1+40=41
1+41=42
1+42=43
1+43=44
1+44=45
1+45=46
1+46=47
1+47=48
1+48=49
1+49=50
1+50=51
1+51=52
1+52=53
1+53=54
1+54=55
1+56=57
1+57=58
1+58=59
1+59=60
1+61=62
1+62=63
1+63=64
1+65=66
1+67=68
1+68=69
1+69=70
1+70=71
1+71=72
1+72=73
1+73=74
1+74=75
1+75=76
1+76=77
1+77=78
1+78=79
1+79=80
1+80=81
1+81=82
1+82=83
1+83=84
1+84=85
1+85=86

```
1+86=87
1+87=88
1+88=89
1+89=90
1+90=91
1+91=92
1+92=93
1+93=94
1+94=95
1+95=96
1+96=97
1+97=98
1+98=99
1+99=100
```

Chapter Thirteen
Mathematics For Children Part Two

$1 \times 1 = 1$
$1 \times 2 = 2$
$1 \times 3 = 3$
$1 \times 4 = 4$
$1 \times 5 = 5$
$1 \times 6 = 6$
$1 \times 7 = 7$
$1 \times 8 = 8$
$1 \times 9 = 9$
$1 \times 10 = 10$
$1 \times 11 = 11$
$1 \times 12 = 12$
$1 \times 13 = 13$
$1 \times 14 = 14$
$1 \times 15 = 15$
$1 \times 16 = 16$
$1 \times 17 = 17$
$1 \times 18 = 18$
$1 \times 18 = 18$
$1 \times 19 = 19$
$1 \times 20 = 20$
$1 \times 30 = 30$
$1 \times 40 = 40$
$1 \times 50 = 50$
$1 \times 60 = 60$
$1 \times 70 = 70$
$1 \times 80 = 80$
$1 \times 90 = 90$

$2 \times 2 = 4$
$3 \times 8 = 24$
$4 \times 44 = 174$
$4 \times 55 = 220$
$5 \times 55 = 275$
$5 \times 556 = 2780$
$6 \times 7 = 42$
$6 \times 66 = 396$
$7 \times 99 = 693$

7×55=385
8×8=64
8×9=72
9×7=63
10×10=100
11×11=121
14×20=280
44×45=1,980
34×33=1,122
12×24=288
94×95=8,930
95×96=9,120
66×100=6,600
77×78=6,006
666×666=443,556
777×777=603,729

1-1=0
1-2=1
3-3=0
4-5=1
6-6=0
7-7=0
8-9=1
9-9=0
10-25=15
13-45=32
14-55=41
15-65=50

10÷50=0.2
11÷70=0.157142857142
1÷3=0.333333333333
3÷7=0.428571428571
4÷4=1
6÷6=1
7÷7=1
8÷8=1
9÷9=1
10÷10=1
11÷11=1

Being Happy Is Good A Poem For Children Written By Professor MCGOKU305

Being Happy Is Good
Being Happy Is Great
Being Happy Is Beautiful
Being Happy Is Bliss
Being Happy Is Harmony
Being Happy Is The Root Of All Light
Being Happy Is Joyful
Being Happy Is healthy
Being Happy Is Natural
Being Happy Is Normal
Being Happy Is Good At All Times
Being Happy Is Happy Is Happy Is Happy
Being Happy Is Tunefulness
Being Happy Is melodiousness
Being Happy Is mellifluousness
Being Happy Is mellifluence
Being Happy Is content
Being Happy Is cheerful
Being Happy Is The Key To Life

- Professor MCGOKU305

Love Of Love A Poem For Children Written By Professor MCGOKU305

Love Of Love The Stars Above Baby Doves And Cats And Rats
Dogs In Hats
 Lady's And Gentleman
Boys and girls
Mice and Squirrels
Love Of Love

Love Of Joy
Love Of Love
Love Of Love
Love Of Love

- PROFESSOR MCGOKU305

The happy-go-lucky Ducky
A Nursery Rhyme Written By PROFESSOR MCGOKU305

The happy-go-lucky Ducky Drunk Water From His Uppy Duppy Sippy Cuppy Tuppy
As He Walks He See's a Puppy Name Yuppy And The happy-Go-lucky Ducky
Is Happy And Laughy And Taffy Into a Short Winter Of Drafty After That He Took a Bathy Wathy
and The Happy go lucky Ducky

Got Inside Of His Bed And Went To Sleep
- Professor MCGOKU305

The Young Whippersnapper
A Nursery Rhymes & Poem For Children
Writing By PROFESSOR MCGOKU305

The Young Whippersnapper

 Who Took Themselves a Napper Woke Up and Went To The Store On The Shore As They
Skipped And They Tripped They Seen a Dog With a Zip then They Dog Locked and Tick Tock•d
Up and Down The Block They Seen And Kitchen With a Hawk Watching A Chicken And Then a
Walking Baby Seen A Scrawling Lady Who Just Came Out Of Hades With Shades and Brady's
and Grady's As The Young Whippersnappers Seen a Bell Clapper They Seen Another Napper
Taker Who Was a Faker and a Shaker Who Ate Bear Flakers Baby's and Cats and Small Baby
Rats Are Jumping and Dancing And Soon To Be Prancing They Seen a Duck and Said Yuck
and Huck and Buck and Seen a Talking Transfer Truck Driving By a Ghost Who Was Eating
Burnt Toast and Raccoon Roast The Ghost Couldn't See And They Ghost Couldn't Hear But
The Ghost Didn't Have any Fear Because He Could Fly But Wondered Why Couldn't Make The
Transfer Truck Fly Too As The Young Whippersnapper Went Back To Home They Cooked a
Garden Gnome And Are Him Like a Meal After They Beat Him With The Heal Of a Anvil And
After They Were Done They Had Some Fun But Didn't Play Near The Windmills and the End Of
The Day After They Play The Sky Turned Grey And They Went to Their Homes Glad and Gay
(Happy) And The Next Day They Are Merry and Cherry And Funny As a Bunny That Is A Story
Of Glory
- Professor MCGOKU305

Fun Facts and Tips

In This Poem The Words Hades And Gay
Are Used Here Are The Definitions For Both Words

Hades
Hades (/ˈheɪdiːz/; Greek: ᾍδης Hádēs; ᾍδης Háidēs), in the ancient Greek religion and myth,
is the god of the dead and the king of the underworld, with which his name became
synonymous Hades was the eldest son of Cronus and Rhea, although the last son regurgitated
by his father. He and his brothers, Zeus and Poseidon, defeated their father's generation of
gods, the Titans,

And Here Is The Definition Of The Word
Gay
 The term was originally used to mean
Happy and "carefree", "cheerful", or "bright and showy". Ugly or Stupid or Foolish

In English, the word's primary meaning was "joyful", "carefree", "bright and showy", Glee,
And

These are The Fun Facts and Tips

World Of Peace Land Of Love

A Poem For Children Written And Created By Professor MCGOKU305

World Of Peace Land Of Love

Is a World Where Peace Is Unlimitedly Beautiful And Where Everyone Is Happy
It Is a World Where All People Get a Long World Of Peace Is a World Where Everything Is
Wonderful And Joyful And At Ease And There Is No War No Violence
Where Everything Is Harmony And Bliss

Land Of Love A Land Of All Love
Pure Love Great Love Where Everyone
Has Respect and Love For Each Other
Land Of Love Is a Lovely Place And a Wonderful Place Where All Of The
Little Boys & Little Girls Are In Love With Themselves And Their Childhood Lives and Each
Boy and Each Girl Love's Each Other and Respect Each Other
And All Of The Grown Up Adults Are Happy and Love Each Other and Live Comical and Happy
Lives They All Live In

World Of Peace And The Land Of Love

- Professor MCGOKU305

Goodness and Greatness And Pureness

A Poem For Children Written By
Professor MCGOKU305

Goodness Is Goodness It Is Good To Be Good To Yourself And Whomever Love's You Being
Good To Yourself Is Self Love

Self Love Is The Most Powerful thing And
Strength That Anyone Can Have

That Is Why Goodness Is The Truth And That Is Why Goodness Is The Only Light

Because Goodness To Yourself Is
Extremely Wonderful And Beautiful

Greatness Is The Second Most Powerful
Weapon Against Anybody Evil And Wicked

The Greatness Of The Mind And The Greatness Of The Body And The Greatness Of The Spirit
And The Greatness Of The Soul And The
Greatness Of Being Your Very Own God
 Is All You Need In Life To Be Your Truth And Guidance Along With The Pure Love Of A Family
That Truly Love's And Respect's You

Pureness Is The Third Most Powerful
Weapon That Is Within All Of Everyone
The Purity Of Being Full Of Pureness Is Beautiful And Being Beautiful Is Pureness staying
celibate And A Virgin Is The Most Important Thing To Do About Being Pure and Staying
Pureness Staying Inside Of Purity Is Wonderful There Are Many Ways of Staying Inside The
Realms Of Pureness

Never Using Profanity (Curse Words)
Never Drinking Alcohol
Always Stay a Virgin Celibacy (cælibatus)
Always Get The Correct Amount Of Sleep
Always Eat The Proper And Right Foods
Always Drink Clean Water Forever
Always Exercise And Take Clean Bath's
Always Keep Positive People In Your Life
Always Keep Yourself Happy and Chipper
Always Keep Your Life Happy And Clean
Always Leave Negative People From You

Always Keep Negative People From You

Always Keep Bad Influences Out Of Your Life

Always Keep Positive Influences Into Your Life

Those are The Keys To Staying within
Pureness

By Professor MCGOKU305

- PROFESSOR MCGOKU305

Puppy Love A Poem For Children Written by Professor MCGOKU305

One Day On a Friday Morning One 4 Year Old
Puppy After Taking a Nap From His Off Of His Tiny Feet He Is Walking Down The Street Whilst
Eating Some Leek (Vegetable) As He Crunches and Munches And Scrunches On His Leek
That He Got Last Week At The Creek From a Bird With a Slick Thick Brick Beak
He Thinks And Blinks and Drinks Some Water and Then Eats Some Vanilla Ice Cream And
Then Screams When He See's a Friendly Roasty Toasty Ghost And Skeleton Who Ate a Slice
Of a Rice Watermelon and
 Gave
The Puppy The Other Slices Of
The Rice Watermelon and a Peach Cake and a Beach Cake With a Snow Flake On The Side
For a Slide As a Ride On a Tide
As The Little Puppy Comes Back Home He See's a Cute Little Female Puppy
With a Uppy Rubber Ducky Cuppy

Her Favourite Healthy smoothie
 Inside Of It

Banana And Strawberries and Raspberries Blue Berries and Black Berries and Plums As She
Jumps And Flumps and Slumps on The Drum With a Sum Of Fun She Thinks Then She Winks
Her Eye And Smiles As She Barks Like Shaks
At The

Happy Little Male Puppy

He Then Runs Over With A 4 Leaf Clover in a Range Rover To Come Over To The
Girl Puppy He Has a Crush On and As He Says

Male Puppy: I Like You

And The Female Puppy Says Back

Cute Female Puppy: I Like You Too

And The Male Puppy Replies Back

Male Puppy: I Got a Crush On You

And The Female Puppy Replies Back

Cute Female Puppy: I Have a Crush On You Too

And The Male Puppy Replies Back Saying

Male Puppy: Want To Bark Bark Be My Bark Bark Girlfriend

And The Female Puppy Replies Back Saying

Cute Female Puppy: Yes I Will Bark Bark
Do You Bark Bark Want To Be My Bark Bark Boyfriend

and The Male Puppy Replies Back By Saying

Male Puppy: Yes i Bark Bark Want To Be Your Bark Bark Boyfriend

And The Two Puppies Lived Happily Ever After As Boyfriend and Girlfriend Puppies

The End

Fun Facts and Tips

Here Is The Definition Of The Term
Puppy Love

puppy love
intense but relatively shallow romantic attachment, associated with adolescents

Puppy love, also known as a crush, is an informal term for feelings of romantic or platonic love,
often felt during childhood and adolescence. It is named for its resemblance to the adoring,
worshipful affection that may be felt by a puppy.

The term can be used in a derogatory fashion, presuming the affair to be shallow and transient
in comparison to other forms of love. Sigmund Freud, however, was far from underestimating
the power of early love, recognizing the validity of "the proverbial durability of first loves".

Characteristics
Puppy love is a common experience in the process of maturing.[4] The object of attachment
may be a peer, but the term can also describe the fondness of a child for an adult. Most often,
the object of the child's infatuation is someone years older, like a teacher, friend of the family,
actor, or musician, about whom the child will spend their time daydreaming or fantasizing.

A crush is described as a coming-of-age experience where the child is given a sense of
individualism because they feel intimate emotions for a person not part of their own family.

There You Have It The Definition Of Puppy Love I Hope You All Enjoy This Beautifully Written Poem By Yours Truly Professor MCGOKU305

Children Of The Forest a Poem For Children

Written By PROFESSOR MCGOKU305

Children Of The Forest The
Extremely Happy Children Whom Live With Their Parents And Grandparents
The Children Of The Forest
Are Strong Children And Can Run Faster Than Any Train On Tracks and Any Aeroplane In The
Sky That Is Why These Children Love To Eat ice Cream and Pie
And The Best Part Of It All They Never Cry

The Children Of The Forest
The Children Of The Land
The Children Of The Children

These Children Walk Bare Feeted Everyday And Every Night And They
Live In Tree House's And Have Neighbors Whom Are Talking Rabbit's and Cabbits
And Dabbits and Babbits and Crabbits
And Cats and Dogs and Bears and Hogs
And Pigs and Squirrels and Skunks
And Sheep's And Chipmunks And
Opossum and Raccoons and Monkeys
 And Mandrillus Baboon And Chickens
And Many Different Animals
From The Sky's Above And The Underworld's beneath
These Children Of The Forest Never Clean Their Teeth Or beneath Their Feet
And They Are Jolly And Merry As Their Heids Are Hairy As They Ate Little Blue & Green
Cherries They Run Through The Forest Chipper Dipper Lipper Hipper Whippersnapper!" and
Merry

- Professor MCGOKU305

Love And Joy And Tranquility and Peace

A Poem For Children Written and Created By Professor MCGOKU305

LOVE IS STRONGER THAN DETEST
LOVE IS STRONGER THAN HATE
LOVE IS STRONGER THAN EVIL
LOVE IS STRONGER THAN NEGATIVITY
LOVE IS STRONGER THAN ANY EVIL

LOVE IS POWER
LOVE IS STRENGTH
LOVE IS GOOD
LOVE IS GREAT
LOVE IS SELF LOVE
LOVE IS THE TRUTH
LOVE IS THE LIGHT
LOVE IS THE MORNING
LOVE IS THE NIGHT

The Definition Of Love Is This

an intense feeling of deep affection.
 For One's Self

JOY
 a feeling of great pleasure and happiness.

Joy Is Good Because Feeling The Feelings
Of Joy Is A Wonderful And Beautiful Thing Always Keep Yourself Full Of Joy Keep Joyful
Thoughts Into Your Mind And Keep Your Mind Full Of Joyful Thoughts
Keep Yourself With Joyfulness In Your Soul and In Your Spirit and In Your Mind And Body

Tranquility
The Definition Of Tranquility
the quality or state of being tranquil; calm.

Tranquility Is The Purest Way Of Life
Tranquility Is The Most Best Part Of life
Tranquility Is Wonderful And Joyful
Tranquility Is The Greatest Part Of Life

Tranquility Is Everything Good and Right
Tranquility Is Peace and Everything

Peace
The Definition Of Peace
freedom from disturbance; Tranquility

Peace
Is The Main Source Of All Thing's Good
Living In a Peaceful Life Is Gorgeous
Living In a Peaceful Life Is Wonderful
Living In The State Of Peace Is Great

Peace Is The Truth And Peace Is The Light
Peace Is The Power Of The Day And The Night

Love And Joy And Tranquility and Peace

A Poem For Children Written By PROFESSOR MCGOKU305

Blackface Bobby Volume 7: Life Lessons Part Three & Four

Peace & Joy
A Nursery Rhyme & Poem By
Written By Professor MCGOKU305

Peace And Joy
Joy And Peace
Children Enjoying life playing With
Their Toys in Pure Bliss And Joy
Little Boys With Their Action Figures &
Little Girls With Their Baby Dolls

Children Outside With
Slingshots & Ring Pops And Soda Pops
At Peace and At Joy Peace On Earth The
Greatest Worth

- Professor MCGOKU305

Blackface Bobby Volume 7: Life Lessons Part Three & Four

True Love Is Self Love
A Nursery Rhymes
Written By Professor MCGOKU305

True Love Is Self Love That Is More Beautiful Then a Dove Who Else Is In Love With Them
Own self With Their Own Wealth With Their Own Work Own Worth From The South To The
North

 One (1) Two (2) Three (3) And Fourth (4th) That Is You
Number One Love Yourself
Number Two Love You
Number Three Protect Yourself
Number Four Have Respect For Yourself

Love Yourself

True Love Is Self Love That Is More Beautiful Then a Dove Who Else Is In Love With Them
Own self With Their Own Wealth With Their Own Work Own Worth From The South To The
North

True Love Is Self Love That Comes From
Inside Of You
That Is From You
That Is Part Of You
That Is Of You
That Is The Most Wonderful Part Of You
Self Love Is The Real Love That Is Birthed From You That Is Birthed From You That Is Birthed
From You

Self Love Comes From Your Spirit
Self Love Comes From Your Soul
Self Love Comes From Your Mind
Self Love Comes From Your Brain
Self Love Comes From Your Body

Always Love Yourself

Life Lessons Part 3 & 4
The Final Chapters Was Only Made To Educate The Children Readers A
On Raising Their Children Better And This Series Dose Contain Dark Ele
Elements and Violent Themes And Various Situation's That Involves
Scammers , Pick-Pocketers , Tricksters
Profanity Use But It Is Only For Educational Purposes Only

 But They Are Only Added To Let Parents and Children That In Real Life
The Present Day That We Live In Today That There Are Evil People In Th
Prey On Children
To Do All Kinds of Wicked and Evil Vicious Things
 And Kidnap Children And Hurt
Children Of Any Age and If Any Parents Are Reading This Now I Want yo
Your Children An Explain To Them About Everything In This Book
And Please Let Them Know Everything Buy Explaining To Them in a Und
The Dangers If This World And The Dangers Of The Evil People Whom li
Pleased Do This To Protect The Lives That You Love
Your Children And Yourself and Never Let Your Child or Children Go Any
Without You Around Them a With Them Or Without a Mobile Telephone c
Screen Telephone Ok
- Professor MCGOKU305

Make Sure To Write Me With Your Fanmail
By Email @

ProfessorMCGOKU305@Gmail.com
ProfessorMCGOKU@Gmail.com

Thank You Kindly My Fans

Blackface Bobby and His Parent Father Blackface

BLACKFACE BOBBY BY MCGOKU305

BLACKFACE BOBBY BY MCGOKU305

HEY THERE KIDS THIS IS
BLACK BOBBY EVEN THOUGH THIS IS THE FINAL VOLUME OF MY FABLES SERIES
DON'T WORRY I WILL BE BACK I WON'T BE AT SCHOOL FOR LONG EVERYBODY OKAY

I WILL BE RETURNING WITH A BRAND NEW SERIES KNOWN AS

THAT IS RIGHT KIDS I WILL BE BACK BUT BETTER THEN EVER
IN MY VERY OWN COMEDY SERIES CALLED BLACKFACE BOBBY COMEDIES. IT WILL
BE A CHILDREN'S FANTASY COMEDY HUMOUR SERIES OKAY KIDS BYE I AM OFF TO
SCHOOL

Fan Mail To Professor MCGOKU305

Hey Everyone This Is PROFESSOR MCGOKU305 And I Want To Hear From All Of You Whom Purchased My
Blackface Bobby Books Thank You For All Of Your Support

Email
ProfessorMcgoku@gmail.com
ProfessorMCGOKU305@Gmail.com

Social Media
Instagram.com/ProfessorMCGOKU305
Instagram @ProfessorMCGOKU305

https://www.facebook.com/ProfessorMCGOKU305/

Facebook @ProfessorMCGOKU305

Follow Blackface Bobby On Instagram
Instagram @TheRealBlackfaceBobby